I0451865

Divided in Land But Together in Heart

PRAISE FOR *STORYSHARES*

"One of the brightest innovators and game-changers in the education industry."
– Forbes

"Your success in applying research-validated practices to promote literacy serves as a valuable model for other organizations seeking to create evidence-based literacy programs."

- Library of Congress

"We need powerful social and educational innovation, and Storyshares is breaking new ground. The organization addresses critical problems facing our students and teachers. I am excited about the strategies it brings to the collective work of making sure every student has an equal chance in life."
– Teach For America

"Around the world, this is one of the up-and-coming trailblazers changing the landscape of literacy and education."
- International Literacy Association

"It's the perfect idea. There's really nothing like this. I mean wow, this will be a wonderful experience for young people."   - Andrea Davis Pinkney, Executive Director, Scholastic

"Reading for meaning opens opportunities for a lifetime of learning. Providing emerging readers with engaging texts that are designed to offer both challenges and support for each individual will improve their lives for years to come. Storyshares is a wonderful start."
- David Rose, Co-founder of CAST & UDL

Divided in Land But Together in Heart

Kugu Soykan

STORYSHARES

Story Share, Inc.
New York. Boston. Philadelphia.

Divided in Land But Together in Heart

Copyright © 2022 by Kugu Soykan

All rights reserved.

Published in the United States by Story Share, Inc.

The characters and events in this book are fictitious. Any similarity to real persons, living or dead, is entirely coincidental.

Storyshares
Story Share, Inc.
24 N. Bryn Mawr Avenue #340
Bryn Mawr, PA 19010-3304
www.storyshares.org

Inspiring reading with a new kind of book.

Interest Level: High School
Grade Level Equivalent: 4.0

9798885979160

Book design by Storyshares

Printed in the United States of America

Storyshares Presents

1

"Quick, get under the bed!" my mother whispered. My father was at war, so only my mother and little sister were home. We all squished under the bed. Outside, we could hear screaming and gunshots. I could feel how scared the two of them were. Another gunshot, and the window broke. A bullet went right into the mattress above us.

I don't know how long we stayed there. The sun leaked from the room and it became dark. Finally, my mother told us to slowly get out from under the bed. She whispered to us to escape through the back door. There was a small hole in the bottom of our fence. My little sister went through it easily. Then it was my turn.

It was a little harder for me. But I got past the fence. I wondered how my mother would get through. When it was her turn, she got stuck. The metal from the fence was going into her skin. My little sister and I were too weak to pull her through. Then a hand appeared.

I was too tired and scared to see who it was. That hand helped pull my mother through the fence. Then, that hand took us to their home, where we hid together.

2

The next time I opened my eyes, the sun was out. We had fallen asleep at my neighbor Yildiz's house. *She was the helping hand!*

Yildiz's ancestors, or past family, are from Turkey. Mine are from Greece. My mother and Yildiz have known each other for all their lives. They went to school together. They went shopping together. They *were* very good friends.

But because of the war, they hadn't been able to talk for months. The military was everywhere now, watching everyone's moves. Making sure we followed their rules.

The war was happening because of politics. Both the Greeks and the Turks had invaded Cyprus with hopes for a greater empire. More land, and more people.

We were all separated from our friends and family now.

3

The next morning, we said our goodbyes to Yildiz and her family. The military was separating everyone to one of two sides. The Greeks were to go to the south. The Turks were to go to the north. We weren't allowed to take anything with us. The government would be assigning us a house and that is where we would live.

A few hours later, we walked into what would now be our home. The house was about the same size, and like ours, every corner was filled with memories. Only these ones belonged to some other family.

I went upstairs to find my new room. It was a little bigger than my old one. The bed was in the center, with a studying table against one wall. There was a bookshelf full of Turkish books that I couldn't read.

I wanted my old life back.

I sat on the bed and heard a crunching noise. When I stood back up and peeled back the sheets, I found an envelope. I opened it up quickly and saw that it was written in English. Thankfully, I knew how to read English, since it was taught at schools in Cyprus. It said:

Dear friend,

My name is Şerife. I am 14 years old. My grandfather is from Turkey. I used to live in this room. Now I will live somewhere in the north. This war is terrible. I will have to switch schools, make my home somewhere else, and find new friends. Worst of all, I don't know when my father will come back. He is at war. I am sure yours is too. I hope all this ends soon. I have written my new address below so we can write to each other, if you'd like.

I hope to hear from you,

Şerife

4

I hid the letter under my pillow so I wouldn't get in trouble.

"Cipriana! Come down for dinner!" called my mother. The day had gone by so fast. It was already dark outside again.

As we ate dinner, my mother told us about the new Buffer Zone the United Nations had made. It was a large strip of land that would separate the north and south. It was meant to be a region of peace between the two sides.

I wasn't really listenining all that well, though. I had the letter on my mind. I wanted to tell my family about it, but I didn't want them to get in trouble.

Once dinner was finished, I ran upstairs to write Şerife a reply.

Dear Şerife,

My name is Cipriana. I am 15 years old. My great grandmother is from Greece. Your old room is now my room. Don't worry, I will take care of everything. I am also very upset about this war. I know nothing about this new place. I hope we can meet up one day. My mother told me that the UN has made a Buffer Zone between us. Maybe after school on Friday, I can come there and we can talk?

I hope to see you,

Cipriana

A few weeks passed before I worked up the nerve to tell my mother that I wanted to walk around a little bit. I had my letter hidden in one hand, and a bit of money.

She told me to stay very close to our new home, but once I was out of her sight, I ran to the border. There, I saw a messenger going into the Buffer Zone.

"Hello, sir, are you going to the north?" I asked.

"Yes, I am. What do you need?"

I gave him the letter I wrote, along with the money. Once I was sure he passed to the north, I ran home.

Divided in Land But Together in Heart

5

The day was finally here. Friday. I had school to go to, but afterwards I would go to the buffer zone to hopefully meet Şerife.

The morning went by very slowly. The afternoon too. All the teachers and students were still trying to get accustomed to this whole new system forced on us. I still had trouble finding everything. But finally...

RINGGGG

The last bell of the day rang and I slipped away from the crowd. I slowly made my way to the buffer zone, making sure I didn't catch anyone's attention.

Once there, I waited for about 10 minutes, which I spent overthinking everything. *Was this really smart? What if Şerife didn't turn out to be the person I thought she would be?*

A few minutes later, a girl with dark brown hair and a pink headband walked up to me. She was still in her navy blue school uniform. She seemed hesitant, like me, or maybe a little shy, so I asked her if she was Şerife. Thankfully, she was.

We sat and talked about our new homes and how we missed our old ones. How we hoped our fathers would return home safe. How we hadn't seen our friends for weeks now because of the separation.

Şerife and I felt we needed to do something. *But what?*

"Do you have a music program at your school?" she asked.

"Yes, why?" I answered.

She explained to me that maybe we could hold a concert in the buffer zone. This way, we could reunite both sides! Even if it would just be for a few hours.

The plan seemed simple enough. Şerife would find a singer and I would find some students to play the drums, guitars, and any other instruments we could find.

We agreed to create posters written in both Greek and Turkish, which we'd hang all over Cyprus. The concert would be the following Friday, just one week later.

It was starting to get late, so with our plan solidly formed, we said our goodbyes and went back to our divided sides.

Divided in Land But Together in Heart

6

The following week, I worked hard on finding people in the music program at my school who would play in the concert. I hung posters all across our side of the buffer zone. They all read in big letters, "Cyprus Bi-Communal Concert".

Şerife and I met once again, and organized a play list of common songs from both languages. That's how we would unify, or bring together, both sides.

As the day grew closer, I got more and more excited. I just *knew* this was going to bring so many people together.

At last, Friday came. After school, I went to the buffer zone with some classmates to prepare for the concert. I was glad to see Şerife was there with her classmates too.

Together, we set up all the instruments and put out chairs. I set out the pastelaki (honey and sesame seeds shaped into bars) my mother had made for everyone.

When I'd first told her about Şerife, she'd been very angry with me for disobeying her rule to stay close to home. And for not telling her about the letter I'd found in my room. But she admitted that our idea was a good one.

Şerife put out the kataifi her sister had made. Kataifi is an almond and walnut pastry in syrup.

Slowly, people started to show up from both sides.

As the musicians played their instruments, everyone shared in food, stories, and dance. Old friends and new came together.

The sun set, and the people of Cyprus sang and laughed together, united and peaceful at heart.

7

Our concert was a beacon of hope and a spark of revolution from the people of Cyprus.

* * *

The laws are more relaxed now, and people from both sides can go to school together and pass through the buffer zone.

Nicosia, the capital of Cyprus, remains the only divided capital city in Europe.

We hope with each generation that the people of Cyprus will become more and more united, just like they were before the war.

About The Author

Kugu Soykan is the author of *Divided in Land & Together in Heart: A Tale of Cyprus*. Kugo was born in Cyprus, and has been living in the United States since the age of two.

About The Publisher

Story Shares is a nonprofit focused on supporting the millions of teens and adults who struggle with reading by creating a new shelf in the library specifically for them. The ever-growing collection features content that is compelling and culturally relevant for teens and adults, yet still readable at a range of lower reading levels.

Story Shares generates content by engaging deeply with writers, bringing together a community to create this new kind of book. With more intriguing and approachable stories to choose from, the teens and adults who have fallen behind are improving their skills and beginning to discover the joy of reading. For more information, visit storyshares.org.

Easy to Read. Hard to Put Down.

www.ingramcontent.com/pod-product-compliance
Lightning Source LLC
Chambersburg PA
CBHW071230170626
46809CB00005BA/2014